THE MOMMY MAKEOVER MURDERS

By Joaquin Mann

This book is dedicated to the
lovers of dramatic stories about
balancing experiences and emotions.

THE MOMMY MAKEOVER MURDERS

Written By
Joaquin Mann

Fullcover Design By
Sun Child Wind Spirit

Edited By
Mylia Tiye Mal Jaza

THE MOMMY MAKEOVER MURDERS

Softcover ISBNS: 057532239X & 9780575322394
Hardcover ISBNS: 246999537X & 9782306790779

Author Contact
Joaquin Mann
Facebook.com/JoaquinMann
writersconsortium@bepublished.biz

Self-Publishing Associate
BePublished.Org - Chicago
Dr. Mary M. Jefferson
(972) 880-8316
P.O. Box 8324
Jackson, MS 39284
www.bepublished.org
publisher@bepublished.org

First Edition.
Printed In the USA.
Recycled Paper Encouraged.

THE WRITERS CONSORTIUM
www.WritersConsortium.us

TABLE OF CONTENT

Prologue

Samantha Shaw had always been a woman accustomed to perfection. The world adored her sleek, platinum blonde hair, her porcelain skin, and her carefully crafted figure. To her, every inch of her body was an investment—a product that needed constant upkeep and enhancement. A middle-aged widow, she had been through enough hardship to believe that she deserved only the best. For years, she had taken great pride in the image that reflected back at her from the mirror.

But in the depths of her vanity, Samantha was about to meet the one thing that could strip away the polished armor she'd built—an event so shattering that it would change her life forever. A botched plastic surgery would be the first blow, but it was the second—a phone call that would shake her world to its core—that truly began her transformation.

The sterile smell of antiseptic hung thick in the air, mingling with the faint scent of expensive lotions and ointments. Samantha Shaw lay flat on the operating table, her eyes fixed on the fluorescent lights above her head, but her thoughts were elsewhere. It had been a long road to get here, one she had prepared for meticulously. For years, she had sacrificed—hours in the gym, countless beauty treatments, her obsession with remaining young and vibrant. The world revered youth, and Samantha had built her life around the pursuit of it. But now, at forty-five, she was ready for the final step, the one that would perfect what nature had started to fade.

She had been widowed for two years, a sorrow that had hollowed out her soul. But the grief, she had learned, was something that could be patched over, like a tear in fabric. This surgery—the mommy makeover—would be her masterpiece. It would erase the lines, the sag, the signs of aging that made her feel invisible, unworthy of the attention she had once commanded. It was time to regain what she had lost.

"You're going to look fabulous, Mrs. Shaw," Dr. Julian Greer's voice was smooth, almost hypnotic, as he reassured her, standing by her side. His smile was warm, but there was something too practiced about it, a kind of emptiness behind his eyes. Still, she trusted him. She had spent months researching him—Dr. Julian Greer, the top cosmetic surgeon in the country, whose name was synonymous with perfection. She had seen the flawless transformations in the magazine spreads, the glowing reviews from celebrities, the endless testimonials. This was her chance to be the best version of herself again.

Her eyes fluttered closed as the anesthesiologist administered the sedative, a wave of warmth washing over her body, pulling her under. She whispered a small prayer to herself—something her mother had always told her: Beauty is power, and power is everything. With that thought, she surrendered to the darkness.

It was supposed to be simple. Routine. A few nips and tucks, a tightening here and there, the reshaping of what time had taken away. But something went wrong.

Samantha woke slowly, the fog of anesthesia still clinging to her consciousness. Her body felt foreign, too heavy and stiff, and a dull ache pulsed through her chest and abdomen. Her heart raced in a panic as she tried to lift her hands, but they were restrained, tethered by medical equipment. The pain intensified, and she gasped for breath, panic setting in.

"Everything's fine," a voice assured her, but it was distant, detached, as if spoken from across a vast ocean. "Just relax, Mrs. Shaw. The surgery was successful. You're just recovering."

The words did little to soothe her. Something was wrong. She could feel it, deep in her bones. The smooth, youthful face she had expected to see in the mirror—perfect, radiant—wasn't there. She tried to move again, but the disorientation and pain overwhelmed her. And then, as if the world had been flipped upside down, the mask of anesthesia slipped away completely, and the reality of her situation hit her like a freight train.

The reflection in the glass beside her wasn't hers.

"Dr. Greer," she croaked, her voice hoarse, weak. "What happened?"

Days passed in a haze of painkillers, blurry vision, and endless medical checkups. The pain never fully abated, the swelling never quite went down. And with each passing day, her anger grew. Not just at Dr. Greer, but at the world that had led her to this moment. Her life had been consumed by a single pursuit: perfection. Now, in the mirror, she saw only a grotesque mockery of what she had been. Her face, the one thing she had counted on to keep her powerful, to make her desirable, was ruined.

And then, as if the universe was twisting the knife, she received the call that would change everything.

Her son, Zachary—her only child—was dead.

Her world came crashing down all over again. Not only had she been betrayed by the surgeons who promised to give her back her beauty, but now, her son—her flesh and blood—had been living a lie. The grief was unbearable, yes, but it was the humiliation that cut the deepest.

Zachary, the child she had raised, the one she had expected to take care of her in her old age, had chosen a life of crime. It was a revelation that would haunt her in ways she couldn't yet fathom. His death was the ultimate betrayal—a boy she had loved, reduced to nothing more than a criminal whose death had been the result of his own choices.

But the betrayal was far from over. It was just the beginning.

With her beauty stripped away, her son's legacy shattered, and her world disintegrating around her, Samantha Shaw knew one thing for certain: she would have her revenge. The plastic surgery that had promised her a new life had instead turned her into a woman with nothing to lose.

In that moment, Samantha swore to herself—she would burn everything to the ground. Dr. Greer, Michelle Vaughn, and everyone who had played a part in the destruction of her life would pay.

This was no longer just about looks. This was about justice.

And justice, as Samantha would soon learn, had a price.

And she was willing to pay it in blood.

Chapter 1
A New Face

Samantha Shaw's fingers drummed anxiously on the plush armrest of the leather chair as she waited. Her eyes darted nervously to the polished glass doors, through which she could see her reflection, but it wasn't quite her own. Not yet, at least. The glow of the fluorescent lights overhead cast an artificial sheen over her face, but that was nothing compared to the radiance she'd once felt. She had always been meticulous about her appearance, ensuring that her skin was flawless, her hair always freshly styled, and her outfits meticulously curated.

Samantha had spent a lifetime creating an image that was as perfect as possible—flawless, untouchable, and ageless.

And yet, here she was, sitting in a pristine, private clinic, surrounded by high-end décor, waiting for her life to change. Dr. Julian Greer's clinic had been described as a sanctuary for the rich and famous—a place where beauty could be perfected with the touch of a scalpel. Word had it that his work was so precise, so transformative, that even the most discerning celebrities trusted him with their secrets.

Samantha had never been the type to settle for mediocrity. She had spent decades perfecting her outward appearance. The surgical treatments and procedures had become as regular a part of her life as getting a manicure. But as she entered her mid-forties, even Samantha knew that the years were beginning to catch up with her. Tiny lines had started to appear at the corners of her eyes, and her cheeks didn't sit quite as high as they once had. Gravity was inevitable, but it was a reality she couldn't quite accept. Not yet.

The decision to go to Dr. Greer had been carefully considered. She'd heard stories of miraculous transformations—clients who left looking like an entirely new version of themselves, youthful and glowing with vitality. She wasn't looking for drastic change.

She simply wanted to restore what time had taken from her. A little lifting here, a little smoothing there. A little nipping, a little tucking.

Samantha had always believed that beauty was power, and that youth was the currency of that power. In a world that worshipped youth, a woman her age had to fight twice as hard to be seen. She refused to let herself become invisible, hidden behind the wrinkles and age spots that were starting to betray her carefully curated image. If she could afford the best, why not take advantage of it?

When the door to the consultation room opened, Samantha's breath caught in her chest. There he was—Dr. Julian Greer, the surgeon who had created some of the most desirable faces in Hollywood. His confident stride and sharp suit screamed authority, but it was the way he looked at her—appraising, almost predatory—that made her heart flutter. She stood quickly, extending her hand with practiced grace.

"Mrs. Shaw, it's a pleasure," he said smoothly, shaking her hand with a firm, deliberate grip. He was tall, dark-haired, with an aura of undeniable self-assurance. "I've heard great things about you."

"Thank you," she replied, her voice cool but edged with excitement. "I've heard nothing but praise for your work. I'm ready for a transformation."

Dr. Greer smiled, his eyes flicking over her with professional interest. "Let's take a look," he said, motioning for her to sit in front of the full-length mirror that spanned one wall of the room.

Samantha sat down, straightening her back, trying to look as poised as possible. She knew this was it—the moment that would define the next chapter of her life. The scalpel would be the tool, and she, the canvas.

"Now," Dr. Greer said as he leaned in to examine her features closely. His fingers gently pressed at the lines around her eyes and mouth, as though he could feel the years in her skin. "You're in great shape. But we can certainly refine what time has left behind."

Samantha nodded eagerly. "I want to look like I did ten years ago," she said, her voice low, almost as if she were admitting a secret. "Just a little younger, a little fresher. But still... me."

Dr. Greer's lips quirked into a subtle smile. "Of course. That's the key—subtlety. We'll lift the jawline, tighten the skin, perhaps a bit of volume around the cheeks. It'll take some time for everything to settle, but I'm confident you'll love the results."

Samantha felt a rush of anticipation flood her chest. She could already picture herself walking through the door of a gala, her flawless face turning heads, the whispers of admiration surrounding her. She would be the envy of every woman, the object of desire for every man. It would be like the clock had been turned back, and she could reclaim the confidence of her youth.

"What do you think, Samantha?" Dr. Greer's voice broke through her thoughts. "Are you ready?"

The question hung in the air for a moment, and she met his gaze. His eyes were calculating, focused—he saw something in her, something he could work with.

Samantha had always been good at seeing what she wanted and getting it. And right now, she wanted this. She wanted this more than anything.

"I'm ready," she said, her voice firm, her heart racing with excitement. "Let's do it."

The days that followed were a blur of consultations and preparations. Samantha was determined to keep herself calm and composed, even as the dread of the procedure loomed over her. She tried to ignore the flicker of doubt that occasionally crept into her mind. This was going to be a big change—physically and emotionally—but she had made her choice. Dr. Greer's reputation had been flawless, and if anyone could restore her to perfection, it was him.

When the day of the surgery arrived, Samantha entered the clinic with the same meticulousness she always had, her heels clicking against the smooth marble floors. She wore a fresh, vibrant smile, eager for the new face that would soon reflect back at her. But something in her gut told her that this would be no ordinary transformation.

And when she woke up from the anesthesia, the pain was more intense than she had anticipated. The bandages wrapped around her face felt like a straitjacket, heavy and tight. Her skin burned beneath them. The rush of panic was instant. It wasn't supposed to hurt like this. It wasn't supposed to feel... wrong.

Her hand trembled as she reached up to touch her face. Her fingers found the swollen contours of her cheeks, the uneven skin beneath her fingertips. Panic set in. This wasn't how it was supposed to be. Her face was swollen, unrecognizable, her once-lush lips stretched tight, and her eyes barely visible under the bandages. Her skin, once taut and porcelain, now sagged unevenly. The sharpness she had once prided herself on was replaced with something distorted. How could this be? She wanted to scream, but her throat felt raw. She could barely breathe, let alone call out.

She called out, her voice thick with confusion and fear. "Dr. Greer? What happened? Something's wrong. Something's—"

But the room was empty. But the room was silent. No comforting voice. No answer. She heard the quiet shuffle of footsteps retreating down the hall, the faint echoes of distant laughter from the clinic's staff as they went about their business, oblivious to her distress.

A wave of dread washed over her, cold and suffocating. Something was horribly wrong. The last thing she could remember was being reassured that everything would be fine. But now? Now, she felt more like a victim than the empowered woman she had dreamed of becoming.

The door creaked open, and a nurse came into view. Her face was kind, but her eyes were filled with that same empty look that had clouded Dr. Greer's expression.

"You're awake," the nurse said gently. "Don't worry. Dr. Greer will be in to see you soon."

The words did little to soothe her. Something was wrong. She could feel it, deep in her bones. The smooth, youthful face she had expected to see in the mirror—perfect, radiant—wasn't there. She tried to move again, but the disorientation and pain overwhelmed her.

"Everything's fine," a voice assured her, but it was distant, detached, as if spoken from across a vast ocean. "Just relax, Mrs. Shaw. The surgery was successful. You're just recovering."

Samantha wanted to demand answers, but her body was sluggish, unresponsive. She reached up toward her face, touching it gently, feeling the rough texture of the stitches beneath her fingertips. The swelling was still there, but something else too— something worse. And then, as if the world had been flipped upside down, the mask of anesthesia slipped away completely, and the reality of her situation hit her like a freight train. She couldn't place it at first, but then it hit her with sickening clarity.

Her beauty—her carefully crafted identity—had been destroyed. Her fingers felt things on her face that should not be there. And now, the reflection she blurry sees in the glass beside her wasn't hers by any means. Only the pain she could see in her eyes were recognizable, all her other emotions felt different.

By the time Samantha's face was finally revealed, it was nothing like the image she had imagined. It wasn't the youthful, flawless appearance she had dreamed of—it was a lopsided, swollen version of herself, twisted and strange. Something had gone horribly wrong. But it wasn't just the surgery that was about to ruin her life. It was the call she would receive next—the call that would shatter everything.

Chapter 2
The Phone Call

The days following the surgery felt like an endless haze. Samantha had spent the first few days after the operation in a state of disbelief, her world shifting between the sharp, searing pain of recovery and the numbing realization that her face—the very thing that had always been her greatest asset—was now a swollen, misshapen version of itself. She had known surgery would bring some discomfort, but nothing had prepared her for the extent of it. It was as if her very identity had now been married to a monstrous mistake in a single stroke, and the lines of time and beauty twisted beyond willful recognition.

This was a pain unlike anything ever experienced. Knowing her 7-Figure husband left the majority of money to charities and mistresses was just another thing that allowed his death to be Samantha's secret joy despite the crocodile tears falling on the matching purse and shoes at the funeral and internment as she clung closely to her son – periodically reassuring him that his father is better off and they will be just fine, so he doesn't need to worry and should move back home to live on the second floor.

But her reflection, hidden behind layers of bandages, mocked her nonchalance about failing to capitalize off her husband's death as planned (and her devotion to bettering her son's life regardless of his own desires and actions). Each time she caught a glimpse of herself in the mirror. The once flawless features and possibilities to marry a billionaire that she had prided herself on seemed so far out of reach now. She had always been the picture of elegance— polished, composed. The kind of woman who made heads turn without even trying. But now, in her vulnerable state, she had become a joke. A grotesque parody of the woman she once was.

Samantha lay in her bed, staring at the ceiling as the sound of a distant television reached her ears from the other room. The house, once a sanctuary of peace and beauty, now felt like a cold shell, echoing with emptiness. Zachary—her only son—was out with friends, as he usually was on weekends, and Samantha had hoped he would visit her after the surgery to offer some reassurance. He hadn't yet come. The silence in the house was suffocating.

But that wasn't unusual. Zachary had always been independent. A sharp, charismatic young man who had grown into someone with a presence that commanded attention. He had followed his own path, sometimes walking the line between rebellion and ambition. But Samantha had never worried about him—not in the way most mothers did. She had raised him to be strong, to stand on his own two feet. She trusted him to make his way in the world.

Still, she had been hoping for some comfort. Some reassurance that things would return to normal once her face had healed. But the swelling showed no signs of retreating. And now, in the dim light of the room, she realized that she couldn't hide from the reality anymore. She had paid for perfection, and she had received something that felt far from it.

The phone rang, snapping her out of her spiraling thoughts. She blinked, her heart beating faster. It was an unfamiliar number, one she didn't recognize. Curiosity momentarily distracted her from the discomfort of her physical appearance.

"Hello?" she answered, her voice scratchy from the anesthesia.

"Mrs. Shaw?" a voice said, cold and professional. "This is Detective Miller with the Los Angeles Police Department. I'm afraid I have some tragic news."

Samantha's heart stilled in her chest. Tragic news? The words reverberated in her mind, leaving her feeling cold. She sat up slightly, her pulse quickening.

"What's happened?" she asked, her voice tight, betraying none of the panic she felt rising inside her.

"There's been an incident involving your son, Zachary Shaw," the detective continued. "I'm afraid we have reason to believe he's been involved in a criminal enterprise—a sex trafficking ring. He was one of the key players. The operation was just recently busted by authorities."

The police had raided a high-end brothel, and in the process, uncovered a shocking discovery. Zachary had been operating a sex trafficking ring, and he had been killed in a bloody standoff with law enforcement during the bust.

Samantha's mind went blank. Her chest tightened. "What are you talking about? Zachary? My son?" Her voice faltered. She couldn't process the words. They didn't make sense. Zachary was... he was a bright, promising young man. He couldn't have been involved in something like that.

"I'm sorry, Mrs. Shaw," the detective said, his tone unyielding. "But we've found evidence linking your son to the ring. It appears he was running operations for the group, and we've gathered information from several sources. He was killed in the bust."

There was a slight pause before he added, "We're still piecing everything together, but his death was part of the police takedown. He didn't survive the raid."

Samantha's mind reeled. The words blurred together, creating a nightmarish fog that made her want to scream. "No," she whispered, her voice hoarse with disbelief. "That can't be true. He wouldn't do that. My son wouldn't be involved in anything like that."

"I understand this is difficult, but we'll need to ask you some questions regarding his possible involvement. We need to determine how deep his connection went. We'll be in touch, Mrs. Shaw," Detective Miller said, his tone suddenly colder, professional once again.

Before she could say anything more, the line went dead.

The phone slipped from her trembling fingers, falling onto the bed beside her. She sat in stunned silence, the weight of the words crushing her chest. Her son. Her only child. The bright, ambitious young man who had been so full of promise—now linked to a criminal enterprise, and now dead. Killed in a police raid.

It couldn't be real. Zachary had always been a good kid. He wasn't a criminal. She had raised him better than that. He'd had dreams. Big dreams. He had wanted to become an entrepreneur, to start his own company. But what if... what if those dreams had taken a darker turn? What if he had been involved with people who had taken advantage of him? Samantha's mind swirled with thoughts of denial, but also of doubt.

Her thoughts were interrupted by a sharp sting in her chest, as though her very heart had cracked open. She gasped, clutching at her chest. The pain was sudden, visceral, as if the universe had taken everything from her in one ruthless stroke.

She could feel the bile rising in her throat, but she swallowed it down, forcing herself to breathe. Slowly. Deeply. This couldn't be happening. It couldn't.

But it was.

Her thoughts turned cold and calculating, a feeling that was unfamiliar but not unwelcome. She had always been in control of her life—of her body, of her career, of her appearance. But now, in the wake of Zachary's death, Samantha felt the first stirrings of a darker, more powerful impulse. She wanted to know the truth. She wanted to understand what had happened to her son.

But not just that. She wanted justice. She needed it. She had lost everything—her son, her beauty, her sense of control. And the surgeons who had botched her face... they were the first ones she would make pay.

As the day wore on, Samantha's grief shifted from numbness to a slow-burning rage. Her son was gone, and now, her own life seemed to have been derailed beyond recognition. She had always lived for herself, had always sought to perfect her image, her body, her life. Now, as the searing pain in her chest seemed to bleed into her every thought, she realized that this would not be the end. This was just the beginning.

The beginning of something far more dangerous. And the first target on her list would be those who had betrayed her—

those who had stolen her son's life, and those who had destroyed her face.

Samantha would not stop until she had answers. And she would not stop until she had her revenge.

Her world had changed forever.

Chapter 3
Descent Into Madness

The days after the phone call passed in a blur of rage, confusion, and disbelief. At first, Samantha had tried to stay composed, holding on to the thread of normalcy that she had once so carefully woven. But the world had shifted beneath her feet, and now, she found herself grasping for something—anything—solid. Her son was dead, caught up in a world of crime she couldn't fathom, and the identity she had so meticulously crafted for herself was falling apart. The betrayal of it all gnawed at her insides.

Her face, still swollen and grotesque from the botched surgery, served as a constant reminder that everything was falling apart. Every time she passed a mirror, she recoiled at the stranger who stared back at her. She had gone in expecting perfection, expecting a flawless reconstruction of her youth, and had emerged a monster. But that wasn't the worst of it. No, the worst part was the revelation about Zachary. The thought that he—her only son—could have been involved in something so vile was unbearable.

She tried to rationalize it. Tried to tell herself that he had been coerced, tricked, or caught up in something he couldn't escape. But the more she thought about it, the angrier she became. The anger bubbled up in her chest, swirling like a dark storm, filling the empty spaces inside her. She had lost her son, her beauty, and now, it seemed like her entire life had been turned upside down.

And that anger—its raw, burning intensity—became her only constant companion.

One morning, as the haze of grief began to recede, Samantha found herself standing in front of her bathroom mirror, staring at her reflection. The bandages were gone, revealing her new face in full, but all she could see was a wreck. There was no longer any trace of the woman she had once been— the woman who was confident, admired, sought after. The face staring back at her now was hollow, distorted by the swelling that still lingered, by the obvious signs of botched work.

Her fingers trembled as they touched the hard, tight skin of her jawline. The cheek implants had been too large. Her nose seemed to have been altered more than she had agreed to. Nothing was right. And it wasn't just her face—it was her entire existence. She felt as though she had been erased and replaced with something far more grotesque.

Her phone buzzed on the countertop, snapping her out of her reverie. The caller ID read "Detective Miller."

Samantha's heart skipped. She hadn't wanted to hear from the police again. The implications of Zachary's involvement in the sex trafficking ring were too much to bear. But she couldn't avoid the call.

"Hello?" she answered, her voice shaky despite her best efforts to sound composed.

"Mrs. Shaw," the detective's voice was gruff. "I know this is difficult, but we need to speak to you in person. We have new information about your son's death. It's important."

Samantha's blood ran cold. She had barely begun to process the fact that Zachary was gone, that he had been involved in something so dark. The thought that there could be more—a deeper layer to the story—was almost more than she could handle.

"I—I don't want to speak to you," she said, the words tumbling out before she could stop them. "I don't want to know anything more. My son is dead. That's enough."

"Mrs. Shaw, please," the detective insisted. "You need to hear this. We're not sure how involved he was in the criminal operations, but we think there's more to it. We have evidence that suggests he was part of a much larger network. We need your cooperation."

Samantha clenched her jaw, her hands shaking with the rising tide of anger and helplessness. How dare they bring her into this mess? How dare they make her relive it over and over again? She had already lost him—her only child. She had no desire to uncover the darkness that had taken him away from her.

"I'll think about it," she said tersely, hanging up the phone before the detective could say anything more.

Her thoughts were now consumed with one thing: revenge.

The rage that had been simmering inside her for days, weeks, finally found its outlet. She was going to make the people responsible for her son's death pay. She would make them feel the same helplessness, the same torment that she had felt when she learned of his involvement in the trafficking ring. She would destroy them the way they had destroyed her life.

But it wasn't just the criminals who had hurt her. It wasn't just the shadowy figures behind the trafficking network. It was the doctors. The surgeons who had taken her money, her trust, and in return, had destroyed the one thing she had always valued: her appearance. They had promised her perfection, and they had given her a monstrous reminder of her own vanity. They had ruined her, just as surely as the people behind Zachary's death had.

The anger swelled again, this time without the fog of grief to dull its edge. It was sharp, focused, and it was turning her into something she didn't recognize. But in that moment, she realized that it didn't matter. She had nothing left to lose.

Samantha started to make a list in her mind. She would need information—about the surgeons, about their backgrounds, their schedules. She would need to find out who had been involved in her surgery, who had made the decisions that had ruined her face. And once she knew who they were, once she had them in her sights, she would make them pay.

But that wasn't all. She had a new mission now. Zachary's death couldn't go unpunished, either. The people behind his involvement in the trafficking ring would pay the price, as well. And Samantha Shaw, once the epitome of grace and elegance, would become the instrument of their downfall.

She wasn't just going to fix her face, fix her body. She was going to fix everything that had been broken. But more than that, she was going to make sure that the people who had hurt her—who had taken her son from her and marred her perfection—would never hurt anyone again.

And so, Samantha set out on her new path, her mind consumed with dark thoughts of revenge. Every step she took, every ounce of energy, was now directed at one singular goal: vengeance.

She wasn't the grieving mother anymore. She wasn't the woman who had once been obsessed with beauty. She had become something else—something cold, something ruthless. She was going to hunt them down, piece by piece, and tear their world apart.

Her journey was just beginning, and she would make sure that every single person who had wronged her would feel her wrath.

Chapter 4
Craving Revenge

The following weeks passed in a blur of research, meticulous planning, and an undercurrent of raw, seething determination. Samantha's world had shifted from one of superficial concerns—her appearance, her social standing—into something far darker. Revenge had taken root inside her like a poisonous seed, and it was growing, twisting through her every thought, every action. She had once been driven by the desire for beauty, but now, beauty was irrelevant. She no longer cared about the perfect lines of her jaw or the sculpted cheeks she'd once dreamt of. No. Now, her focus was singular, her goals clear: the people who had destroyed her life, her son's life, had to pay.

The botched surgery still tormented her. Every day she could feel the disfigurement— she ran her fingers over the stiff, lumpy contours of her face, where once had been smooth, youthful skin. But her anger at the surgeons was no longer just about vanity. It was personal. They had taken her money, her trust, and ruined the one thing she had believed defined her. But as much as they had hurt her, the pain of losing Zachary was worse. The call from Detective Miller still echoed in her mind. The thought that her son, the boy she had raised, had been involved in such dark dealings, was like a constant ache deep in her chest.

Samantha's first step was to investigate Dr. Julian Greer and his team. She had learned that the clinic he ran was a well-oiled machine, catering to the rich and famous, offering high-end cosmetic procedures with promises of perfection. But beneath that glossy surface was a far darker reality. It didn't take long for her to uncover discrepancies in the clinic's history—multiple lawsuits, questionable practices, and rumors of botched surgeries that had been swept under the rug.

Greer's reputation, polished with the help of influencers and high-profile clients, hid a tangled web of malpractice. Samantha spent countless hours in front of her computer, poring over articles, public records, and online forums, uncovering the names of people who had been dissatisfied with their surgeries—patients whose lives had been ruined, just like hers. Some had even died during or after their procedures, but the deaths were always covered up, silenced by the power of the clinic's wealthy clientele.

She learned about Dr. Greer's personal life, his colleagues, and his assistants—each piece of the puzzle adding to the picture of a man who was far from the talented, flawless surgeon he presented himself to be. His arrogance was evident in the way he handled disgruntled patients and the complaints that were lodged against him. But there was something else. Something that caught Samantha's attention. One of Dr. Greer's top associates had recently been involved in a scandal—an associate named Michelle Vaughn, who had vanished after a botched breast augmentation procedure. Samantha dug deeper into Michelle's background, piecing together fragments of information that led her to a shocking revelation: Michelle Vaughn was the person who had performed Samantha's surgery.

A cold fury washed over her as the realization sank in. Michelle had been the one who had destroyed her face. Michelle had been the one who had betrayed her trust, and now, Samantha knew exactly where she needed to start. She had to find Michelle, and she had to make her pay.

The next phase of Samantha's plan was not as simple as finding a name. No, this was far more intricate. She needed leverage. To take down Dr. Greer, to ruin his empire, she needed something he couldn't ignore—a secret, a weakness, something that would bring him to his knees. She wasn't just going after the surgeon responsible for her disfigurement. She was going after the entire operation.

Samantha had learned that the clinic was not only involved in shady procedures but had also been the subject of investigations into illegal organ harvesting. There were whispers in certain circles about patients disappearing—under the guise of medical complications—never to be seen again. Greer and his team had connections in high places, and they were protected. But Samantha wasn't afraid of power or money. If anything, it gave her an edge.

Her first move was to get into the clinic unnoticed. She had worked her way into the world of high-end fashion and business in the past, learning how to manipulate her appearance, her presence, to gain access to the places she wanted to be. She was going to do the same now, but for a different purpose.

She contacted an old acquaintance—someone in the world of exclusive high society, a man named Marcus Langley. He was an influential businessman with ties to both the medical and entertainment industries, someone who could get her into places most people could never reach. Over a lunch that seemed like nothing more than a casual social gathering, she dropped subtle hints about her dissatisfaction with the work done at Greer's clinic. She framed it as a chance encounter, a casual complaint, and Marcus, ever the opportunist, immediately offered to help her get a meeting with Dr. Greer himself.

It was all falling into place.

A week later, Samantha was sitting in the plush, glass-walled office of Dr. Julian Greer. The clinic had arranged for her to meet with him under the pretense of a second consultation. He greeted her with that same, practiced smile—the smile that had once made her feel like she was in the presence of a genius.

"I'm glad you decided to come in again," Dr. Greer said smoothly, his eyes sweeping over her face as if appraising a piece of art. He was good at that—making people feel like they were the center of his world, like their needs and desires were the most important thing in the room. Samantha couldn't help but feel disgusted by his charm, now that she knew the truth.

"I've been thinking about what we discussed," she said, her voice soft and controlled. "I think I need a more thorough revision. Something more... subtle. Something to fix what went wrong."

Greer leaned back in his chair, his fingers steepling in front of his lips as he studied her.

"Of course," he said, his voice smooth. "We'll fix it. You've come to the right place. No one does this better than me."

Samantha could feel her pulse quicken, but she held herself steady. This was the moment. She needed to remain calm, to control the conversation.

"Do you have records of my surgery? I'd like to go over the details," she asked, her voice low, almost sweet.

Greer looked at her quizzically but nodded. "Of course. We keep meticulous records for all of our patients. I'll have my assistant retrieve them for you." He stood up, his movements graceful, confident, like a predator preparing to make its move.

As he turned to leave the room, Samantha's eyes scanned the space around her. The sleek furniture, the polished floors — everything was designed to reinforce his image as the king of his domain. But underneath it all, she knew that the empire he had built was about to come crashing down.

The pieces were falling into place. Soon, Dr. Greer would be exposed. Soon, Michelle Vaughn would face the consequences of her actions. But first, Samantha needed to gather more. She had to ensure that nothing, absolutely nothing, was left to chance.

This was no longer about cosmetic surgery. This was about tearing down a life built on lies. This was about making them all pay for what they had done to her and to Zachary.

The hunt had begun. And Samantha Shaw was a force they would soon come to fear.

Chapter 5
The Aftermath

The meeting with Dr. Julian Greer had been everything Samantha needed it to be— and nothing more. She had played her part well, hiding the rage burning beneath her calm facade, masking the hunger for retribution that simmered just under the surface. As he walked out of the room, she sat in the pristine leather chair, allowing herself a brief moment of reflection.

The sleek, clinical surroundings of his office—the carefully curated art on the walls, the soft hum of the air conditioning—were the perfect backdrop to his polished demeanor. But behind that facade, Samantha knew the truth. Greer's empire of flawless beauty was built on corruption, lies, and malpractice. Every perfect face that had walked out of his clinic carried with it the scars of those who hadn't been so lucky.

Samantha wasn't just a victim anymore. She was the storm that would dismantle everything he had worked for.

Her fingers tightened around the edge of the chair. This wasn't just about payback for her own botched surgery. This was personal. Zachary's death—the circumstances surrounding his involvement in the trafficking ring—were the driving force behind her every action now. The rage she felt for the people who had destroyed her life and taken her son from her was consuming. Greer and his associates had been careless. They had assumed she was just another vain, wealthy woman seeking perfection. They were wrong.

As Dr. Greer disappeared down the hallway to fetch the medical records she'd requested, Samantha's mind raced. It was time to execute her plan, to ensure that every piece of leverage she had would fall into place.

The clinic was busy that afternoon. Several patients were waiting in the luxurious lobby, each one absorbed in their own world of vanity. Samantha's mind snapped into focus as she observed the people around her They were all so eager to put their faith in Dr. Greer, to trust that his hands would give them exactly what they wanted. They were oblivious to the dangers lurking behind those glass walls. But Samantha wasn't.

She glanced at her watch. Her assistant, Marcus Langley, would be arriving soon. He had arranged for her to get the meeting with Dr. Greer, but that wasn't enough. She needed more information. She needed a way to make sure that once the trap was set, Greer and his entire clinic would crumble beneath her.

In the meantime, she needed to move quickly.

As the minutes ticked by, Samantha felt a sudden rush of adrenaline. She wasn't here just to gather information. She was here to plant the first seed of chaos.

When Greer finally returned with her records, he handed them to her with a professional smile, but Samantha could see the unease flickering behind his eyes. He had no idea what was coming. She could feel the power shifting with every second.

"Here you go, Mrs. Shaw," Greer said, offering the papers with a bow. "As you can see, your procedure was entirely within the standard guidelines. There were no complications. It was a standard facelift and jawline adjustment, with the addition of cheek implants. Everything was performed meticulously."

Samantha scanned the records, nodding as she pretended to take in the information. In truth, her mind was elsewhere—on the security footage she'd secretly obtained of Dr. Greer's team performing the procedures. Marcus, "Mr. Wednesday," had pulled strings to get it for her. The footage showed things that shouldn't have been happening in a professional setting. The team had been distracted, careless, even mocking their patients at times. The video was damning, and Samantha would use it to destroy him.

She looked up at Greer with a soft smile. "I see. But..." She paused, letting her words hang in the air. "What about the issue with Michelle Vaughn? I heard there were complications with some of her surgeries recently. What can you tell me about that?"

Greer's face tightened, a flicker of discomfort passing through his eyes. Samantha knew she'd hit a nerve.

"Michelle was a talented member of my team," Greer said stiffly. "She had a personal issue, which caused her to... step away for a short period. But we have handled that. She's no longer involved with the clinic."

Samantha leaned forward slightly, narrowing her eyes. "Really? Because I've heard rumors, Dr. Greer. That Michelle's... issues... were more than personal. That she was involved in some other procedures that shouldn't have happened."

Greer's gaze shifted uneasily, but he recovered quickly, his polished demeanor back in place. "I assure you, Mrs. Shaw, everything has been taken care of. The clinic is still the leading facility in the city, and I've never had a malpractice suit brought against me. My clients are always satisfied."

Samantha could feel the tension thickening in the room. It was clear Greer wasn't as confident as he appeared, and that was exactly what she wanted to see. The cracks in his perfect armor were beginning to show. She had made her point. The seed of doubt had been planted. But she wasn't done yet.

"Of course," she said softly, standing up. "I'll think about the next steps for my procedure. But, Dr. Greer, I think you should be careful. People talk. Your patients talk, your staff talks. And if you're not careful, something like Michelle's 'issues' might turn into something bigger. Something... irreversible."

She gave him a knowing smile before turning to leave. The air between them had thickened with tension, and Samantha could feel the subtle shift in power. As she walked out of the office, she could feel Greer's eyes on her, but she didn't turn back. This was only the beginning.

Later that evening, Samantha sat in the dimly lit office of her rented space—a secure, high-tech building far removed from the glitzy glamour of her former life. Her fingers flew over the keys of her laptop, analyzing the footage she had from Greer's clinic, cross-referencing it with the documents she had acquired. Every piece of information was now part of a larger puzzle, one that was starting to take shape in ways she hadn't even anticipated.

Marcus Langley, who had become her unofficial partner in crime, had delivered his end of the bargain. He had connections to the world of media and blackmail, the kind of people who could exploit information to their advantage. Together, they had identified the key players who had been complicit in the botched surgeries at Greer's clinic. They had compiled evidence that would leave Greer with no way out.

As she scrolled through the footage of Michelle Vaughn, her rage flared once again. Michelle's face—once confident, now hidden behind the same mask of fear and arrogance Samantha had seen so many times before— was the final piece of the puzzle. She had known that Michelle had been the one who performed her surgery, but now she had everything: the tapes, the witnesses, and the other patients who had suffered under her hands.

Samantha's fingers stopped for a moment on the mouse as she stared at the screen, taking in the evidence. She knew what came next.

It was time for the first strike.

Greer's world was about to crumble, and she would be the one to tear it down.

The following morning, an anonymous email was sent to the media outlets. It contained the footage from the clinic—the full, unedited video of the botched surgeries, along with a detailed account of Greer's past malpractice suits. The attached documents included the names of former patients who had suffered under his care, along with the allegations of illegal activities involving organ harvesting and trafficking.

By the end of the day, the clinic's pristine reputation was shattered.

Samantha watched the news unfold from the comfort of her office, the heat of satisfaction curling in her chest. The first piece had fallen into place. Now, it was only a matter of time before Dr. Greer, Michelle Vaughn, and everyone else involved would feel the weight of their actions.

The hunt had begun. And Samantha Shaw wasn't stopping until she had everything she wanted.

Her plan was in motion, and she would make sure no one who had wronged her—no one who had a hand in taking her son's life—would ever escape her justice.

Chapter 6
The VIP Firm

The fallout from the leaked video was immediate and brutal. News outlets were all over the story, with headlines screaming about the corruption and malpractice at Dr. Julian Greer's world-renowned clinic. Samantha sat back in her chair, her eyes flicking over the reports flooding her inbox, a grim satisfaction settling deep in her chest. She had expected this—a media storm of fury and condemnation. What she hadn't expected was just how quickly it would escalate.

The clinic's phone lines were flooded with angry calls. Greer's social media pages were overrun with posts accusing him of everything from negligence to outright criminal activity. Within hours, the medical boards were calling for investigations, and lawsuits were being filed by former patients who had suffered under his care. Michelle Vaughn, the surgeon who had worked on Samantha's face, was nowhere to be found. Rumors spread that she had gone into hiding, but Samantha wasn't concerned about her just yet. She had dealt the first blow, and it had landed with devastating impact.

But this was just the beginning. Samantha's victory wasn't complete. Greer and his team had resources—money, power, connections. They would fight back. It was time to escalate.

By evening, Samantha had made the necessary arrangements. She had contacted Marcus Langley, who had been working behind the scenes, pulling strings and ensuring that the right people were in place. Together, they'd set up a meeting with someone who had the power to take things to the next level.

Marcus was a key player in the world of corporate espionage, and he had connections to people who didn't just deal with the press or the law. No, these were the types of people who dealt with problems quietly— people who could make inconvenient problems disappear without leaving a trace. Samantha was done with playing in the shadows. She wanted to make sure the damage to Greer's empire was irreparable.

The meeting was set in an upscale downtown penthouse, the kind of place where high rollers gathered to discuss serious business away from the public eye. Marcus had arranged for a trusted ally, a former intelligence operative named Samir, to be present. Samir had a reputation for being able to extract information—or people—from the tightest of situations. Samantha had vetted him personally. If anyone could ensure that Greer's empire came crumbling down, it was Samir.

When Samantha arrived, she took a moment to compose herself. The weight of everything she had endured—the pain of losing Zachary, the torment of her disfigured face, the humiliation of having her body turned into an object of scorn—was heavy, but it had also forged a new version of herself. A version who wasn't afraid of blood.

She stepped into the penthouse, the thick carpet muffling her footsteps. The city lights filtered in through floor-to-ceiling windows, casting long shadows across the polished wood floor. Marcus stood near the window, talking quietly with Samir, a tall man with a weathered face that betrayed years of experience.

Samantha approached, her heels clicking on the floor. As she came closer, Marcus turned and gave her a reassuring smile. "Everything's ready," he said. "Samir has the tools we need. Now we just need to finalize our approach."

Samantha's gaze locked onto Samir. He was studying her with cold, calculating eyes. "I assume you've gone over the details?" she asked.

He nodded. "I've seen the footage. Greer's done. But the real question is how far you're willing to go to make sure he pays for what he's done. I can get the job done, but it won't be clean."

Samantha's lips curled into a tight smile. "I don't need clean. I need final."

Samir's eyes flickered with approval. "Good. I like when people know what they want."

The plan was simple, but it would be devastating. Samir had a network of informants within the city's underground, people who knew how to access sensitive data, people who could infiltrate the high-net-worth circles that Greer and his associates inhabited. Using a combination of blackmail and threats, Samir would ensure that Greer's most powerful clients—people whose financial backing had kept him safe for years—turned on him. At the same time, Marcus had arranged for several media outlets to be given even more explosive information about Greer's illegal activities, things that had been buried by his powerful connections. Samantha didn't just want to take Greer down. She wanted to destroy everything he had built, to show the world that no one—no matter how powerful—was untouchable.

Samantha's role was far more direct. She had the leverage, and now it was time to use it. She had tracked down the locations of several key members of Greer's team, including the infamous Michelle Vaughn. Using the information Samir had gathered, she planned to confront them directly.

The first stop was Michelle's apartment. Samantha had been following her movements for days, waiting for the right moment. The surgeon had been keeping a low profile since the scandal broke, but she hadn't been smart enough to stay completely hidden. Michelle had a tendency to frequent a coffee shop near her apartment, and it was there that Samantha knew she would find her.

When she arrived at the café, she noticed Michelle immediately. The woman was seated in a corner booth, nervously scanning the room as if she were waiting for someone. Her once-confident posture was gone, replaced by a hunched, defensive demeanor. Samantha could see the fear in her eyes, and she felt a flicker of satisfaction. It wasn't enough that she had exposed Greer. Now she was going to make sure Michelle paid for what she had done to her.

Samantha didn't waste time. She slid into the booth across from Michelle, who jumped slightly at the sudden presence. Her eyes widened when she recognized her.

"Ms. Vaughn," Samantha said, her voice smooth, cold. "We need to talk."

Michelle opened her mouth to speak but hesitated. "I... I don't know what you're—"

"You ruined my life," Samantha interrupted, leaning forward slightly, her voice a low, almost dangerous whisper. "You were the one who performed that surgery. You were the one who took everything from me. You took my son's future, and you thought you could just walk away from it. But I'm not done with you."

Michelle's face went pale as she realized who was sitting across from her. "I... I didn't mean to..." Her voice trailed off, but her words were hollow.

Samantha's lips twisted into a cruel smile. "It doesn't matter. You were part of something bigger than yourself. And now, you'll be held accountable."

Before Michelle could respond, Samantha leaned back, pulling out a small envelope from her bag and placing it on the table. "This is your first warning. If you don't cooperate, if you don't give me everything I want, I'll make sure you never work again. Your reputation is already ruined. Your life will be a lot harder if I release the rest of the footage. You're going to help me destroy Greer, and you're going to make sure you're the one to take the fall."

Michelle's hands trembled as she picked up the envelope, but she didn't speak. She couldn't. She knew it was over. Samantha had won.

"Good," Samantha said, her voice filled with quiet satisfaction. "Now, we can move on to the next phase. And trust me, it's going to be much worse for you if you try to run."

Samantha stood up, leaving the café with a sense of finality. Michelle Vaughn would now be a pawn in her game, just like Dr. Greer, just like the rest of them. The media, the blackmail, the threats—it was all coming together. Samantha had played the long game, and now the empire that had been built on her misery was crumbling before her eyes.

As she walked out into the cold night, she felt a sense of power surging through her veins. The reckoning had begun. Greer and his team were going to fall. And when they did, Samantha Shaw would be there to pick up the pieces of their shattered lives, ready to make them all pay for the pain they had caused her.

But the game wasn't over yet. The final moves had yet to come. She'd learned a lot during her marriage to Big Zach.

And Samantha was just getting started with issuing recompense.

Epilogue

The city had settled into an uneasy quiet in the wake of the destruction that had been unleashed by Samantha Shaw. Greer's clinic was a husk of what it had once been—its name tarnished beyond repair, its once-glamorous clients now fleeing in droves, desperate to avoid being linked to the scandal that had nearly ruined them. The media frenzy had died down, but the legal battles continued, dragging out in courts that no longer cared about Greer's pristine reputation.

The surgeons who had been complicit in the botched surgeries, including Michelle Vaughn, were facing charges of malpractice, negligence, and even human trafficking. The clinic itself had been seized by federal authorities as part of an investigation that spanned across multiple states.

And then there was Samantha, who had managed to slip away from the chaos with the quiet grace of a woman who had already moved beyond it. Beyond it all, including her 24 years with Big Zach.

A year had passed since the downfall of Dr. Julian Greer and the complete dismantling of his empire. The dust had settled, and yet, for Samantha, there was no sense of closure. She had won, yes, but victory had a strange way of leaving a hollow feeling in its wake. She had taken down the system that had wronged her—but there was more to be done. The game had changed, and Samantha had changed with it.

She stood in front of a large glass window in a sleek, modern office that was all angular lines and polished chrome, looking out over the city she had once walked through in a daze of pain and loss. She had rebuilt herself in ways that no one—not even herself—could have imagined. The old Samantha Shaw, the desperate widow whose face was marred by a surgeon's incompetence, was gone. She had forged a new identity, a new purpose, and a new path forward.

In this city of sin and power, she was no longer a victim. She was a force—a corporate vigilante willing to bleed for those who had nowhere else to turn.

Samantha had established The VIP Firm—a consultancy firm that operated in the shadows, offering services to those in power who needed a helping hand with their dirty work. With a reputation for getting results at any cost, The VIP Firm quickly became a name whispered in boardrooms, whispered among Big Zach's crew, whispered between the most influential and dangerous figures in the world. Samantha was willing to do whatever it took to get the job done, even if it meant crossing lines that would destroy others' lives.

And yet, she didn't work for just anyone. She had become selective, offering her services only to those who had been wronged in ways that mirrored her own. Her firm's motto, posted in bold letters on the wall behind her desk, read: "Justice for those who can't fight back."

Her gaze softened as she looked down at a series of photos pinned to a corkboard across the room—photos of the people who had been affected by the operations of Greer's clinic, victims who had been torn apart by his greed. Some had found new lives; some had not. Those who had survived the physical toll had often found their lives shattered in other ways. She had made sure that they were compensated in ways that the law could not provide. She had made sure they would never be forgotten.

Her personal revenge had been exacted, but that hadn't been the end. It had just been the beginning of something much more complex, something that went beyond one woman's pain and suffering. There were other villains, those who lured her son into sex trafficking others and ultimately framed him so his life would be taken. There were other powerful men hiding their sins behind shiny facades.

There were other families who had been torn apart by this system that didn't care. And Samantha Shaw had decided that she would be their reckoning. She started by putting all of Zachary's so-called bosses out of breath as soon as she could find them. She never forgot the M16 lesson her father gave her when she was 10-years-old. She eliminated all four of them efficiently and silently, walking away without a spot of their blood on her.

The door to her office opened, and Marcus Langley stepped inside, holding a tablet in his hands. He was one of the few people Samantha had kept close over the past year, a partner in crime, so to speak. He was Big Zach's go-to man, his Boy Friday now her Mr. Wednesday. His loyalty, sharpened by the months of work they'd done together, had earned him a place in the inner circle of The VIP Firm. He was more than just a resource; he was a trusted confidant.

"You wanted the report on the Bellamy case?" Marcus asked, his voice smooth, always calculated.

Samantha didn't immediately respond. She turned her gaze from the window to meet his eyes, her face a mask of quiet confidence. "I've been thinking about something else," she said, her voice calm but with an edge of something sharper, something dangerous beneath it. "I'm done playing the game from the sidelines. I've made my name—now it's time to make my mark on the world."

Marcus raised an eyebrow, curious but unruffled. "And how do you intend to do that?"

Samantha's lips curled into a cold smile. "By becoming the one thing they all fear. A corporate avenger. There are too many systems out there—too many powerful men and women who think they can do whatever they want. They think they can hide their sins behind money and status. They think they can get away with murder. I've had enough of watching them win. I'm used to my fingernails being painted red!"

Marcus set the tablet down on her desk, leaning forward slightly. "So you're saying… you want to expand the firm?"

Samantha nodded slowly. "Not just expand it. I want to build an army."

The next few months were a whirlwind of growth and strategic maneuvering. Samantha's firm gained a reputation not only for solving problems but for solving them in ways no one could have imagined. She was no longer just a consultant; she had become an enforcer in the world of high-stakes business and politics.

Her network expanded, bringing in ex-intelligence officers, disgraced corporate lawyers, and individuals who operated on the fringe of the law. Her team operated with precision, attacking her targets where they were most vulnerable—exposing their darkest secrets and leveraging them to bring about their downfall. She didn't need to break laws to make them pay. She simply exposed their weakness and let the world do the rest.

But Samantha didn't let the power go to her head. She remained focused on the mission—on the people who had no voice, on the innocent victims who had been crushed by the system. The VIP Firm became a sanctuary for those who had nowhere else to turn, a place where the broken could be made whole again, and the powerful could be brought to their knees.

As Samantha stood in her office overlooking the city once more, she felt a quiet sense of fulfillment. Her vengeance had been sweet, but it wasn't enough. Not anymore. She had transcended the need for personal revenge. Now, it was about rewriting the rules of power itself, creating a world where the broken could rise again, and where the guilty would never be allowed to hide.

In the reflection of the glass, she saw herself—a woman remade, standing at the helm of something far greater than she had ever dreamed. The woman who had once been nothing more than a widow with a broken face who buried her infamous child, now stood as an unstoppable force—a corporate vigilante, and the architect of a new power structure that shapes the world she sees to fit her order.

And in that moment, Samantha Shaw knew with unshakable certainty that her story was just beginning but she has to take time out to treat herself to something delectable for jobs well done – as well as assure she keeps her Mr. Wednesday just where she has him (stashed to the side and ready to ride on command).

"Maybe a little whiff will do some good," she giggled as she walked to her bedroom, fell back onto her bed, and fantasized about Marcus standing there in chocolate glory as the cityscape glistens and teases behind him.

The Art & Artist

Published with assistance from BePublished.org in March 2025, THE **MOMMY MAKEOVER MURDERS** by Joaquin Mann delivers a twisted, high-octane thriller that will keep you on the edge of your seat from the first page to the last. Samantha Shaw, a vain, middle-aged widow, undergoes a

botched plastic surgery that leaves her disfigured and devastated. But when a shocking revelation reveals her only son's death — linked to his involvement in a dangerous sex trafficking ring — the veneer of her privileged life shatters completely.

Fueled by grief, rage, and a burning thirst for revenge, Samantha embarks on a brutal spree of retribution, targeting the surgeons and individuals who ruined her life. The stakes rise as she unravels a web of corruption, exposing the dark underbelly of the beauty industry. When the dust settles, Samantha walks away with a staggering windfall and a reputation that will make even the most powerful men and women tremble.

As Samantha emerges from the ashes of her shattered life, she reinvents herself as the head of "The VIP Firm" — a corporate vigilante group willing to take on the world's most powerful corrupt figures, all while keeping their hands bloody and their motives personal.

THE MOMMY MAKEOVER MURDERS is a chilling tale of revenge, resilience, and ruthless ambition. Perfect for fans of dark thrillers, gripping mysteries, and female-driven narratives, this book will leave you questioning the price of perfection and the lengths one woman will go to for justice.

"I wanted to do something unexpected, so while I was working on my science-fiction series, this popped up," the 51-year-  old graphic designer and voice-over artist maintains. "Coming from behind the scenes to manifest my own vision for myself had to happen. I'm glad I finally prioritized my dreams and did for myself what I had been doing for others all these years. I hope you all like mine just as much too."

Enjoy **THE MOMMY MAKEOVER MURDERS** by Joaquin Mann today — because no one gets away with murder . . . or with making Samantha Shaw a victim.

Available as a Kindle ebook worldwide, **THE MOMMY MAKEOVER MURDERS** by Joaquin Mann is also available for order as softback book and hardcover book from bricks-and-mortar and online book retailers including your favorite local bookstore, Amazon and BePublished.org.

Facebook.com/JoaquinMann